To Virginia

Special thanks to:
Francis Morrone, Nancy Paulsen, Cecilia Yung and
The Brooklyn Museum of Art Library

Copyright © 1999 by Keith DuQuette

Published simultaneously in Canada. Printed in Hong Kong
by South China Printing Co. (1988) Ltd.
Book design by Marikka Tamura. Text set in Quorum Medium

Library of Congress Cataloging-in-Publication Data
DuQuette, Keith. The house book / Keith DuQuette.   p. cm.
Summary: Rhyming text celebrates the many parts of a house,
from the floor and its welcome mat to the walls, windows,
stairs, and roof. [1. Dwellings—Fiction.   2. Stories in rhyme.]
I. Title.   PZ8.3.D928Ho   1999   [E]—dc21
98-15820   CIP   AC
ISBN 0-399-23183-8
1 3 5 7 9 10 8 6 4 2
First Impression

THE
HOUSE
BOOK

Keith DuQuette

G. P. Putnam's Sons • New York

How does a house come to be
a place to live for you and me?

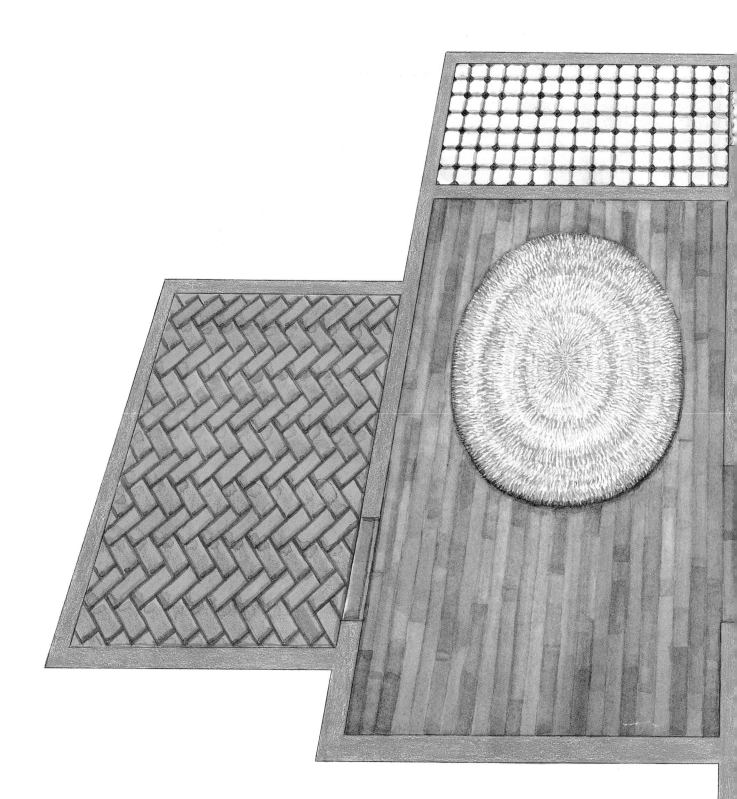

A house is made of many parts;
the floor is where the story starts.

Spreading out and lying flat;
carpet, tile, welcome mat.

From the floor the walls arise,
giving rooms their shape and size.

Swinging open, sliding free,
doors invite in company.

But if they're closed up with a lock,
then you'll have to knock, knock, knock.

Windows show the world outside;
when it's hot they open wide.

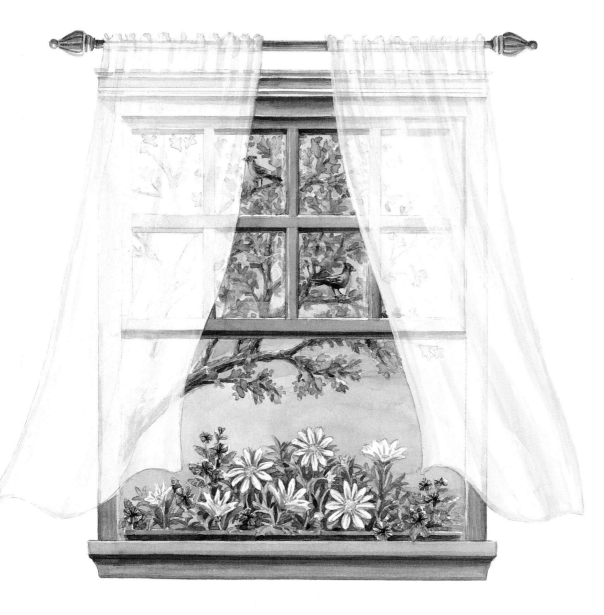

But when it's cold out shut them tight;
and still enjoy the day's warm light.

Step by step, up and down,
stairs will get us off the ground.

You could say that climbing flights
helps us reach much higher heights!

Each room is used in its own way,
some for work and some for play.

Another fact that's worth revealing;
one room's floor's another's ceiling.

Roofs are needed, there's no doubt,
for keeping falling objects out.

There's even more to be seen,
around each home and in between.

In lively cities and quiet woods,
houses make our neighborhoods.

Houses of all shapes and styles,
from town to town for miles and miles.

You've seen the things that houses do,
but they're not homes without you.

Walt Disney's

The GRASSHOPPER
and the ANTS

RETOLD BY Margaret Wise Brown

ILLUSTRATED BY Larry Moore

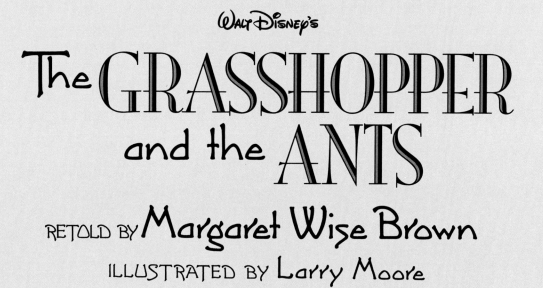

Disney
PRESS

NEW YORK

This text originally appeared in the collection entitled *Little Pig's Picnic and Other Stories*,
published by D. C. Heath and Company.

"The World Owes Me a Living"
from the Walt Disney Silly Symphony
"The Grasshopper and the Ants."
Words by Larry Morey. Music by Leigh Harline.
Copyright © 1934 by Bourne Co.
Copyright Renewed.
International Copyright Secured. All Rights Reserved.
Used by Permission.

Library of Congress Catalog Card Number: 93-70938
ISBN: 1-56282-534-8 / 1-56282-535-6 (lib. bdg.)

The GRASSHOPPER
and the ANTS

Oh, the world owes me a living,
Tra la la lalala la.
The grasshopper was singing his song as he jumped through the fields.

He almost jumped on top of some ants who were pulling grains of corn up an anthill.

Said the grasshopper to the ants: "Why are you working all through the day? A summer day is a time to play!"
"We can't," said the ants. "Winter will soon be here."

The busy little ants did not have time to feel the warm summer sun or to run and jump just for fun. From the beginning of day till the end, they were busy hauling the corn away. Winter was coming. They had no time to play.

All summer the grasshopper sang and danced his grass-hopper dances in the grasses. When he was hungry, he reached out and ate.

And the grasshopper sang:
The good book says: "The world provides.
There's food on every tree."
Why should anyone have to work? Not me!
Oh, the world owes me a living, tra la la lalala la.

With that, he took a big swig of honey from a blue harebell that grew above his head. Then he spit a big wet spit of grasshopper tobacco juice. It nearly landed on a little ant who was dragging a load of cherries to store in the ant house for the winter.

Said the grasshopper to the ant:
    The other ants can work all day.
    Why not try the grasshopper's way?
    Come on, let's sing and dance and play!
    Oh, the world owes me a living, tra la la lalala la.

The little ant was so charmed by the music that he dropped his heavy load and started to dance.

Then came the queen, the Queen of All the Ants.

   And the Queen of All the Ants frowned on the dancing ant so that he picked up his cherries and went back to the other busy ants. The Queen of All the Ants spoke sober words to the grasshopper: "You'll change your tune when winter comes and the ground is white with snow."

But the grasshopper only made a courtly bow.
"Winter is a long way off," he said. "Do you dance?
Let's go."

Oh, *the world owes me a living, tra la la lalala la.*
The other ants can work all day.
Why not try the grasshopper's way?
Come on, let's sing and dance and play!

But even as he sang and played on his fiddle, the Queen of All the Ants hurried away. She, like the other ants, had no time to play.

All through the long, lazy summer months the grasshopper went on singing:

Oh, the world owes me a living, tra la la lalala la.

There was no tomorrow. There was only today, and the sleet and the snow seemed far away.

But the little ants worked harder than ever. As long as the sun was in the sky, they went back and forth carrying the foods from the fields into their ant house.

Then the winter wind began to blow. It blew the leaves off all the trees. The ants ran into their ant house and closed the door, and you didn't see them in the fields anymore. Every day the winds would blow. And then one day–SNOW.

The grasshopper was freezing. He couldn't find any leaves to eat. All he had was his fiddle and his bow. And he wandered along, lost in the snow. He had nothing to eat and nowhere to go. Then far off he saw one leaf still clinging to a tree.

"Food! Food!" cried the hungry grasshopper, and he leaned against the wind and pushed on toward the tree. But just as he got there, the wind blew the last dry leaf away.

The grasshopper dropped his fiddle and watched the leaf go. It fluttered away through the white snowflakes. It drifted slowly away. It was gone.

And then he came to the house of the busy ants. He could hear them inside having a dance. They had worked hard all summer, and now they could enjoy the winter.

The grasshopper was too cold to go on. The wind blew him over, and he lay there where he fell. His long green jumping and dancing legs were nearly frozen. Then, very slowly, he pulled himself through the snow to the house of the ants and knocked.

When the ants came to the door, they found him there, half frozen. And ten of the kind and busy ants came out and carried the poor grasshopper into their house. They gave him hot corn soup. And they hurried about, making him warm.

Then the Queen of All the Ants came to him. And the grasshopper was afraid, and he begged of her: "Oh, Madam Queen, wisest of ants, please, please, give me another chance."

The Queen of All the Ants looked at the poor, thin frozen grasshopper as he lay shivering there. Then she spoke these words: "With ants, just those who work may stay. So take your fiddle—and PLAY!"

The grasshopper was so happy that his foot began beating out the time in the old way, and he took up his fiddle and sang:

> I owe the world a living, tra la la lalala la.
> I've been a fool the whole year long.
> Now I'm singing a different song.
> You were right, I was wrong. Tra la la lalala la.

Then all the ants began to dance, even the Queen of All the Ants.

And the grasshopper sang:
  Now I'm singing a different song.
  I owe the world a living, tra la la lalala la.

Margaret Wise Brown

(1910–52) wrote more than one hundred books for children, including *Goodnight Moon* and *The Runaway Bunny. The Grasshopper and the Ants,* one of several stories she wrote for The Walt Disney Company, was discovered in the Disney Archives. Her stories and poems continue to touch the lives of countless children.